This is Hairdresser Hannah.
She is the best hairdresser
for miles around.

A catalogue record for this book is available from the British Library

Published by Ladybird Books Ltd
80 Strand London WC2R 0RL
A Penguin Company

2 4 6 8 10 9 7 5 3 1

© LADYBIRD BOOKS LTD MMIV

Illustrations © Emma Dodd MMIV

LADYBIRD and the device of a Ladybird are trademarks of Ladybird Books Ltd

All rights reserved. No part of this publication may be reproduced,
stored in a retrieval system, or transmitted in any form or by any means,
electronic, mechanical, photocopying, recording or otherwise,
without the prior consent of the copyright owner.

To Rebecca love from Santa xxx

Little Workmates

Hairdresser Hannah

by Ronne Randall
illustrated by Emma Dodd

"Scissors and snips, curls and clips!" sang Hairdresser Hannah as she opened her salon.

She was especially cheerful today because Queen Clara was coming in for a perm!

Hairdresser Hannah carefully set out all her equipment – scissors, combs, brushes, shampoo, lotion, curlers and clips.

"I have to have everything ready and waiting for Queen Clara!" she said to herself.

At ten o'clock, Queen Clara arrived.

"Good morning, Your Majesty," said Hairdresser Hannah.

"Good morning, Hannah," said Queen Clara. "I hope you can make me look extra special for my garden party today."

"First, I'll wash your hair," said Hairdresser Hannah. "Please take off your crown, Your Majesty."

"Crumbs! I forgot I was wearing it!" Queen Clara laughed.

Hairdresser Hannah worked up a thick, bubbly lather with the shampoo.

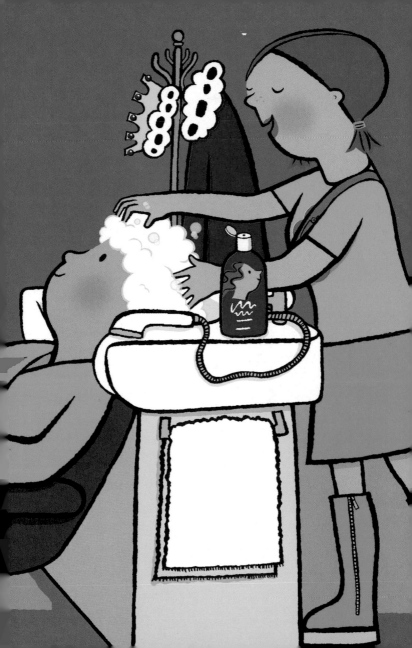

Next, Hairdresser Hannah put on special perm lotion. "It's a brand new and improved lotion," she told Queen Clara. "It's supposed to be the best!"

"That's good," said Queen Clara, "because I have to look my best today!"

"Curlers and clips!" said Hannah as she set Queen Clara's hair on rollers. "You'll have the loveliest curls in Story Town, Your Majesty."

Queen Clara smiled.

Queen Clara read a magazine while her hair dried.

After a while, the timer buzzed.

"Your perm is finished!" said Hairdresser Hannah. "Let's see those beautiful, bouncy new curls!"

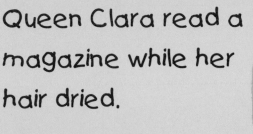

"Oh! Snipping scissors!" fretted Hairdresser Hannah when she saw the Queen's hair. "It must be that new perm lotion!"

"Crumbs! Cripes!" exclaimed Queen Clara when she looked in the mirror.

Queen Clara's hair was curly—but it was also green!

"Oh, my goodness!" said Queen Clara. "The garden party is in just one hour! Whatever will I do?"

"Maybe your crown will hide it," Hannah said. But the crown only covered part of Queen Clara's green hair.

Suddenly, Hannah had an idea. "I'll be right back!" she said.

Hairdresser Hannah
rushed next door to
her neighbour, Florist
Fern.

"I need your help!"
she said. Then she
told Fern her idea.

"I'd be delighted to
help!" said Florist Fern.

In a few minutes, Hairdresser Hannah was back with some pretty red flowers. She put them in Queen Clara's hair.

"Now your hair is a flower garden!" she said.

"What a clever curly creation!" said Queen Clara. "Perfect for a garden party!"

Hairdresser Hannah was the guest of honour at Queen Clara's garden party.

Everyone thought Queen Clara looked wonderful – PC Polly and Nurse Nancy both said they wanted garden hairstyles too!

Footballer Fabio

Vet Vicky

Doctor Daisy

Builder Bill

Postman Pete

Fireman Fergus

Nurse Nancy